STAMPEDE OF THE GIANT REPTILES

DINOSAUR COVE™

DINOSAUR COVE™

STAMPEDE OF THE GIANT REPTILES

by
REX STONE

illustrated by
MIKE SPOOR

Series created by
Working Partners Ltd

OXFORD
UNIVERSITY PRESS

With special thanks to Jan Burchett and Sara Vogler

Thank you, also, to Mark Ford of the British and Irish Meteorite Society for his patient and helpful advice.

For Grandpa Dillon R.S.

These illustrations are for you Christopher.
Enjoy the adventure! M.S.

OXFORD
UNIVERSITY PRESS

Great Clarendon Street, Oxford OX2 6DP
Oxford University Press is a department of the University of Oxford.
It furthers the University's objective of excellence in research, scholarship,
and education by publishing worldwide in

Oxford   New York

Auckland   Cape Town   Dar es Salaam   Hong Kong   Karachi
Kuala Lumpur   Madrid   Melbourne   Mexico City   Nairobi
New Delhi   Shanghai   Taipei   Toronto

With offices in

Argentina   Austria   Brazil   Chile   Czech Republic   France   Greece
Guatemala   Hungary   Italy   Japan   Poland   Portugal   Singapore
South Korea   Switzerland   Thailand   Turkey   Ukraine   Vietnam

Oxford is a registered trade mark of Oxford University Press
in the UK and in certain other countries

© Working Partners Limited 2008
Illustrations © Mike Spoor 2008
Eye logo © Dominic Harman 2008

Series created by Working Partners Ltd

Dinosaur Cove is a registered trademark of Working Partners Ltd

The moral rights of the author have been asserted

Database right Oxford University Press (maker)

First published 2008

British Library Cataloguing in Publication Data

Data available

ISBN: 978-0-19-272097-9

5 7 9 10 8 6 4

Paper used in the production of this book is a natural,
recyclable product made from wood grown in sustainable forests.
The manufacturing process conforms to the environmental
regulations of the country of origin.

FACT FILE

➡ JAMIE HAS JUST MOVED FROM THE CITY TO LIVE IN THE LIGHTHOUSE IN DINOSAUR COVE. JAMIE'S DAD IS OPENING A DINOSAUR MUSEUM ON THE BOTTOM FLOOR OF THE LIGHTHOUSE. WHEN JAMIE GOES HUNTING FOR FOSSILS IN THE CRUMBLING CLIFFS ON THE BEACH HE MEETS A LOCAL BOY, TOM, AND THE TWO DISCOVER AN AMAZING SECRET: A WORLD WITH REAL, LIVE DINOSAURS! BUT THE BOYS HAVE TO WATCH OUT FOR FALLING OBJECTS AND STAMPEDES!

JAMIE

- **FULL NAME:** JAMIE MORGAN
- **AGE:** 8 YEARS
- **SIZE:** 1 JATOM*
- **TOP SPEED:** 10 KPH
- **LIKES:** FOSSIL HUNTING AND LEARNING ABOUT DINOSAURS
- **DISLIKES:** BEING STUCK INDOORS

Jamie's eye

Jamie's foot

Jamie's hand

*NOTE: A JATOM IS THE SIZE OF JAMIE OR TOM: 125 CM TALL AND 27 KG IN WEIGHT

TOM

- **FULL NAME:** THOMAS CLAY
- **AGE:** 8 YEARS
- **SIZE:** 1 JATOM*
- **TOP SPEED:** 10 KPH
- **LIKES:** TRACKING ANIMALS AND EXPLORING WILDLIFE
- **DISLIKES:** RAINY DAYS

Tom's eye

Tom's hand

WANNA

- **FULL NAME:** WANNANOSAURUS
- **AGE:** 65 – 80 MILLION YEARS**
- **SIZE:** LESS THAN A JATOM*
- **TOP SPEED:** 50 KPH, ESPECIALLY WHEN BEING CHASED BY A T-REX
- **LIKES:** STINKY GINGKO FRUIT AND BANGING HIS HEAD ON TREE TRUNKS
- **DISLIKES:** SCARY DINOSAURS

Wanna's head

Wanna's foot

*NOTE: A JATOM IS THE SIZE OF JAMIE OR TOM: 125 CM TALL AND 27 KG IN WEIGHT
**NOTE: SCIENTISTS CALL THIS PERIOD THE LATE CRETACEOUS

EDMONTOSAURUS

Edmontosaurus's hoof

Edmontosaurus's eye

Edmontosaurus's Teeth

Edmontosaurus's nose

- **FULL NAME:** EDMONTOSAURUS
- **AGE:** 65 – 80 MILLION YEARS**
- **LENGTH:** 10 JATOMS*
- **WEIGHT:** 130 JATOMS*
- **TOP SPEED:** ABOUT 45 KPH ON FOUR LEGS
- **LIKES:** THE FOREST WHERE IT CAN HIDE FROM PREDATORS AND SNACK, TOO
- **DISLIKES:** BEING ALONE. IT PREFERRED TO HANG OUT WITH ITS HERD.

*NOTE: A JATOM IS THE SIZE OF JAMIE OR TOM: 125 CM TALL AND 27 KG IN WEIGHT
**NOTE: SCIENTISTS CALL THIS PERIOD THE LATE CRETACEOUS

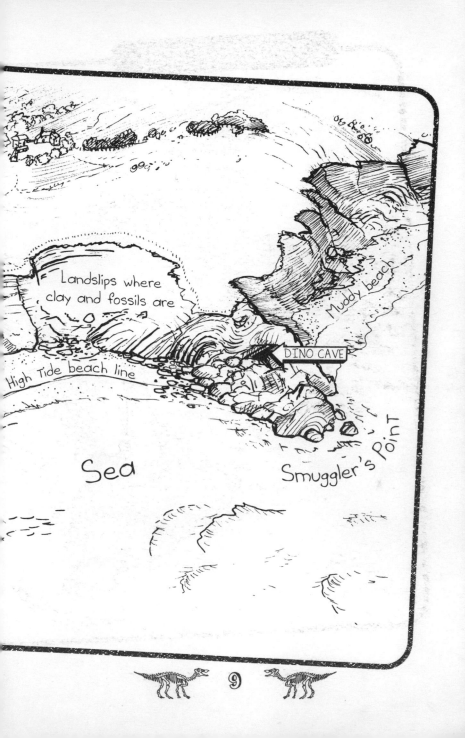

Landslips where clay and fossils are

Muddy beach

DINO CAVE

High Tide beach line

Sea

Smuggler's Point

CHAPTER 1

Jamie Morgan stared at the huge dinosaur towering over him.

'That is awesome!' he exclaimed to his best friend Tom. 'A life-sized model of an edmontosaurus skeleton.'

The gigantic skeleton only just fitted in the museum on the ground floor of Jamie's lighthouse home. Its huge tail curled round the whitewashed walls and it reared up so that its duck-billed nose was high over the boys' heads. The museum was finally ready.

A big banner hung outside the lighthouse:
**Dinosaur Cove Museum Grand Opening
Today, One O'Clock**. This was the day
everyone had been waiting for.

FLASH! FLASH! FLASH!

Jamie and Tom blinked in surprise. The
photographer from the county paper was
aiming her camera at the edmontosaurus.
They jumped aside.

'It's OK, boys,' she called, waving an arm.
'Let's have you in the shot. It'll show readers
just how big this beast really was.'

She took picture after picture, then grabbed Jamie's dad and made him pose over by the Cretaceous landscape model.

Tom rubbed his eyes. 'I'm seeing stars after all that!'

'But imagine how many photos she'd take if she saw a real live edmontosaurus,' said Jamie.

'We've never seen a real one close up,' said Tom.

'Maybe we will one day,' Jamie whispered.

Jamie and Tom shared an amazing secret. They had discovered Dino World, a land of living dinosaurs, and they visited it whenever they could.

'I wonder why we haven't already seen one,' said Tom.

'This will tell us where to look,' declared Jamie. He turned on his Fossil Finder and typed in: edmontosaurus.

 14

'*HERBIVORE,*' he read from the screen.
'*ATE LEAVES AND BRANCHES. SLOW
MOVING. WALKED ON ITS BACK LEGS—*
just like our model.'

'But where did it
live?' asked Tom.

'It says here it kept
to the trees to hide
from predators. That
was its only defence.'

'That explains why
we've never seen
one,' said Tom, 'if
they were always
hiding. That should
be our next dinosaur mission—hunt
the eddie!'

Jamie put the Fossil Finder away in his
backpack. He had a gleam in his eye. 'Maybe I
could ask if we can have a break?'

Tom grinned. 'Are you thinking what I'm thinking?'

'Time for a trip to Dino World!'

Dad was being photographed next to the triceratops skull so Jamie and Tom ran up to Grandad. He was frowning at his reflection in a display case.

'Look at me,' he said, before Jamie had a chance to speak. 'Why can't I wear my old jumper and trousers like I do every other day of the year? I feel silly all done up like a dog's dinner.'

'But you look so smart in that suit, Grandad,' said Jamie. 'No one will look at the exhibits. They'll all be admiring you.'

'Get away!' Grandad laughed as he straightened his tie. 'They'll just think I'm another fossil. Now what are you two scamps after? Out with it.'

'It's nothing really,' said Jamie casually. 'It's just that, well, the museum's ready now so we were wondering if we could go outside for a while.'

Grandad looked at the ankylosaurus-shaped clock on the wall, showing nine fifteen. 'Don't see why not,' he said. 'As long as you're back sharp at one for the ceremony—clean and tidy.'

'Thanks, Grandad.' Jamie swung his backpack onto his back and hurried out of the lighthouse, Tom right behind him.

They scrambled across the beach and up to the cave entrance high in the cliffs.

Making sure no one was in sight, they slipped inside. Jamie dug in his backpack for his torch, but his hand closed around something lumpy and hard.

'Hey, look,' Jamie said, pulling it out along with the torch. 'This is the ammonite I found on my first day in Dinosaur Cove.'

'The first day we discovered Dino World,' Tom remembered.

Jamie tossed the fossil in his backpack and shone the torch on the five fossilized footprints in the stone floor. Every time he saw them he felt the same rush of excitement.

'Let's get back there,' he said. The boys trod in each of the dinosaur prints.

One ... two ... three ... four ... FIVE!

The dark cave disappeared and they stepped into the scorching heat and dazzling light of Dino World.

'It's great to be back!' exclaimed Tom, looking at the huge trees and dense jungle undergrowth around them.

Instead of the usual hum of insects and distant calls of dinosaurs there was an eerie silence.

'Listen!' Jamie said.

Tom listened hard. 'I can't hear a thing.'

'Exactly,' said Jamie. 'Something's not right.'

CHAPTER 2

'Wanna!' called Jamie. His voice sounded strange, echoing through the silent trees. 'Where are you, Wanna?'

There was no sign of the friendly little dinosaur who usually came to greet them. The boys began searching the undergrowth, pushing aside giant tangled creepers.

There was a rustling in a nearby laurel bush. 'What was that?' Jamie stopped. 'Wanna?'

The little wannanosaurus crept out from between the leaves, his eyes darting about nervously. Jamie and Tom rushed over and hugged him.

'You don't know how pleased we are to see you,' said Tom, scratching him hard on his scaly back.

But Wanna just gave a feeble grunk.

Tom frowned. 'This isn't like you, Wanna. What's the matter?'

Jamie reached up into a tree and picked some orange fruit. 'I know what you need, boy,' he said. He tossed one to Wanna and put the others in his backpack.

Wanna looked warily around and then gulped the fruit.

'One thing hasn't changed,' said Jamie. 'Wanna still loves gingkoes.'

'Another thing hasn't changed,' Tom said, holding his nose. 'The gingkoes are still as smelly as ever.'

'But everything else is different.' Jamie frowned. 'Let's find out what's going on.'

With Wanna sticking close to their heels, they made their way through the jungle to a gap in the trees where they could look out over the Great Plains. The plains lay below them, shimmering in the heat—completely deserted.

'There should be herds of triceratops and

hadrosaurs and loads more,' said Tom in disbelief. 'I don't like it.' He pulled out his binoculars and scanned the plains. 'There's nothing moving at all, except the geyser spouts of course. They're still shooting up into the air.'

'What if the dinosaurs are gone?' whispered Jamie.

Tom looked at him, horrified. 'No, they must be here somewhere.'

The boys started down the steep slope of Gingko Hill, but Wanna hung back, trembling and grunking anxiously.

'Come on, boy,' called Jamie, holding out a gingko from his bag.

The little dinosaur crept forward and ate the fruit. He didn't leave their side as they trampled through the hot, damp undergrowth, and jumped the stepping stones over the river.

'This silence is really strange,' said Jamie in a low voice.

'And I've never seen Wanna like this before,' said Tom. 'Not even when we met the T-Rex!'

Suddenly, there was a deafening crash overhead.

BANG!

The boys ducked instinctively.

BANG! Another one. The boys

dived to the ground, covering their heads

with their hands. Wanna disappeared under
a cluster of spiky flowers.

Jamie raised his head. 'There's no way that
was a dinosaur!' he whispered. 'Not even a
T-Rex could make that much noise.'

'So what could it be?' Tom asked.

CHAPTER 3

Jamie and Tom scrambled to their feet.
'We've got to find out what that was,'
muttered Jamie. 'Here, Wanna!'

A terrified Wanna crept out from the
leaves of his hiding place. The three friends
walked through the last few trees and out
onto the plains.

'Look at that!' gasped Tom.

Two blinding lights, as bright as the sun,
were scorching through the sky over the
Far Away Mountains.

'Meteors!' gasped Jamie, screening his eyes from the glare.

The boys watched as the glowing objects shot towards the middle of the plains like supersonic jets. They left long dazzling trails behind them.

'They're falling to earth!' yelled Jamie. 'And fast.'

'They're going to hit the plains,' shouted Tom.

BOOM!
BOOM!

There was a
dreadful noise like
cannon fire. The ground
shook and the boys and
Wanna were knocked off
their feet.

The trees behind them
shuddered wildly. All at once the
sky was full of pterosaurs screeching
and squawking, and there were calls
from the jungle—deep and
rumbling. Out on the plains, two
columns of dust billowed into
the air where the
meteors had hit.

Jamie and Tom
sat up. Wanna was
still lying on his back,
shaking.

'Cool!' said Jamie.
'We've just seen a meteor strike!'

'And felt it!' said Tom, getting
up and gently pulling Wanna to
his feet. 'No wonder he was so
nervous and all the dinosaurs are
hiding. They must have sensed
the danger.'

The boys scanned the plains from
Fang Rock right round to the cliffs of the
White Ocean. There were still no creatures
to be seen. Even the pterosaurs had
disappeared again.

A look of horror came over Tom's face.
'Don't some people say that it was a meteor

that killed the dinosaurs millions of years ago? Do you think that's going to happen here?'

'No,' said Jamie firmly. 'That one was so huge that it created a massive dust cloud and blocked out the sun. These haven't. But we can find out more about them.' He pulled out his Fossil Finder and tapped in: *METEOR*. Then he read, '*A LUMP OF ROCK FROM SPACE THAT HITS THE EARTH'S ATMOSPHERE WITH A SONIC BOOM...*'

'That must have been the bangs we heard when we were in the jungle,' nodded Tom.

'*AND STREAKS ACROSS THE SKY WITH A BRIGHT GLOW,*' Jamie continued. '*THE ONES THAT HIT THE EARTH ARE CALLED METEORITES*. Look: here are some awesome pictures.'

He showed Tom.

'Wow!' Tom said. 'We could actually see real meteorites—just after they've landed!'

'I've always wanted to see a space rock,' said Jamie. 'Let's head for those dust clouds.'

The boys left the jungle behind them and set off across the vast, grassy plains. Wanna scampered along, looking happier now.

'They've landed a lot further away than I thought,' said Tom. 'One of the dust clouds is right at the foot of the Far Away Mountains —near that pine forest.'

'Then we'll head for the closer one,' said Jamie, 'near where the geysers are.' He pulled out the map they'd made of Dino World. 'That's where we chased the velociraptor.'

'Well, I hope he's not still lurking around!' Tom checked his compass. 'We should head north-west,' he said.

'Shouldn't we be seeing the waterspouts gushing up then?' Jamie shielded his eyes as he peered forward. 'All I can see is steam.'

'The dust must be hiding them,' said Tom.

He held an imaginary microphone.
'And here's Tom Clay taking you on
a quest to find the supersonic
space rocks that have
spooked all the
creatures of
Dino World.'

'I wonder what
Tom Clay has to
say about the
ground ahead.'
Jamie said, pointing.

'It's black!' Tom gasped.
'I mean ... Now we can clearly
see the effects of this meteor strike.
We are entering the blast area now.
All around the vegetation is
singed and ... Wow! I can feel
the heat through my trainers.'

The boys walked gingerly across the blackened earth.

'You're right,' said Jamie. 'It is hot! Look at poor Wanna. He could do with some shoes.'

Their little dino friend was hopping from side to side trying not to get his feet burnt.

'Look!' Tom said, as they came nearer the site of the strike. 'There are little fires all around us.'

Small plants were crackling, sending sparks into the air. A spark landed on a dry bush nearby and it burst into flames.

Wanna skittered off in alarm.

'It's OK, Wanna,' said Tom. 'Stick with us and you'll be fine.'

'The fires will probably have scared off the raptor,' Jamie guessed.

'Good thing for us, because we don't have any bacon to distract it,' Tom said.

The air was becoming very steamy.

'We should have reached the geysers by now,' said Jamie. 'But why can't we hear the water spouting?'

Cautiously
the boys stepped
forward through the steam
and saw a huge, gaping hole.

'This is where the geysers should be,'
Tom said.

They peered over the rim of the pit and
Jamie's feet dislodged stones which
tumbled into the bottomless dark.
They could hear hissing and
rumbling deep
underground.

'It's like being on the edge of a cliff,'
breathed Tom. 'The ground's just . . .
vanished!'

'The meteorite has destroyed the geysers,'
said Jamie in amazement.

'That's some power,' said Tom.
'It must have smashed through the
underground caverns where the water heats
up. Now the geysers can't spout up any more.'

'The hole looks as wide as a football pitch,' said Jamie. 'And who knows how deep.'

Grunk-shoo!

Wanna was sniffing at the edge, sneezing as the steam went up his nose. There was a sound of shifting stones and the ground beneath his feet began to crumble. Earth spilled down into the darkness.

'Get back, Wanna!' cried Tom in alarm. 'It's not safe.'

But it was too late. With a horrible crack, the edge gave way. Wanna didn't even have time to grunk before he disappeared into the deep, cavernous hole.

'Wanna!' yelled Tom.

CHAPTER 4

Jamie dropped to his hands and knees and edged towards the place where Wanna had disappeared. He felt the hot steam on his face as he peered into the blackness. Had they lost their faithful friend?

'Wanna?' Jamie called out tentatively into the dark chasm.

Grunk. The response was soft and frightened, but relief flooded through Jamie. Wanna was still alive!

'I can see him!' Jamie yelled. 'He's stuck on a sort of rock shelf.'

'We've got to rescue him!' Tom exclaimed. Jamie took off his backpack and lay down on his stomach. 'I'll try to reach him.'

Tom held his friend's ankles as Jamie leaned carefully over the hole. Through the steam Jamie could just see Wanna, cowering on the ledge, his eyes wide and terrified. Beyond him was nothing but the dark of the deep, steaming pit.

Quick as lightning, Jamie made a grab for him. His fingers closed around one front leg. 'Got him!'

He felt Tom pulling hard on his ankles and Jamie clung to Wanna with all his strength. Wanna scrabbled on the side of the rock wall, trying to help. Slowly and surely Jamie and Tom hauled Wanna up out of the pit. At last, the three of them lay sprawled on the ground.

'That was close,' Tom said.

The little dinosaur darted between his rescuers, licking their faces.

'I think he's saying thank you.' Jamie grinned.

Grunk, grunk!

Wanna seemed to agree.

'We're not going to find any meteorites in that steam hole,' said Tom. 'Let's check out the other landing site.' He pointed to the dust cloud which was still hovering over the trees at the foot of the Far Away Mountains.

'We haven't been that way before,' said Jamie. 'We'll be able to add what we find to the map.'

'Good idea,' said Tom, checking his compass. 'We're heading north of the geysers, or what's left of them.'

Skirting carefully round the huge pit, the boys set off with Wanna, heading straight towards the Far Away Mountains. As they got closer, the ground around became rougher. They had to step over mossy rocks to reach the blackened earth of the second strike. More plants were crackling around them and they could see that the trees nestling at the foot of the mountains had been scorched by the blast.

There were small fires burning amongst the broken branches.

'On with our mission,' said Jamie. 'Meteorite, here we come.'

'There's the crater,' said Tom. He pointed to a dip in the ground about twenty metres ahead.

'Yay!' Jamie hurried towards it. It was a perfect saucer shape. In the centre lay a jagged black rock, glinting in the sun.

Jamie punched the air. 'It's the meteorite!'

They slid down the gentle slope to the gleaming space rock.

'Awesome!' Tom cheered.

Jamie gingerly reached out a finger to touch the surface. 'It's cold!' he said in surprise. He flicked open the Fossil Finder. *'METEORITES,'* he read. *'FRAGMENTS OF ROCK THAT FALL TO EARTH FROM SPACE. THEY CAN MEASURE FROM A GRAIN OF SAND UP TO A FOOTBALL FIELD.'*

'Wow!' gasped Tom. 'I'm glad this one's not as big as that!' He tried to lift it but it didn't budge. 'It's amazing that it's cold when everything else around here is scorched.'

Jamie scanned his Fossil Finder. 'It says the meteor is only hot when it enters the atmosphere and will have cooled down by the time it reaches the ground. The fires around are caused by the impact when it hits.'

They examined the rock closely. 'It's got shiny pieces of metal in it,' said Tom, running his hand over it. 'And holes like space worms have burrowed through it.'

'Just think,' said Jamie, jumping on top of the rock. 'Less than an hour ago this was hurtling through the galaxy!'

Tom joined him. 'Here's Tom Clay and Jamie Morgan, famous explorers, whizzing past the stars on their own personal meteor.'

'Whoa! There goes Mars!'

'Mind the Moon!'

'Here comes Planet Earth. Crash!'

Jamie jumped off the meteorite and threw himself onto the dusty floor of the crater. Wanna grunked round him, enjoying the fun.

'I'm off to Saturn!' Tom announced from the meteorite. 'Hang on, what's that?' he said seriously, balancing on tiptoe. 'I can see a dinosaur!' He asked Jamie to pass up the

binoculars and then peered towards the
distant trees which were still smouldering
from the meteor strike.

Jamie climbed up beside him. 'What is it?'

Tom handed him the binoculars.

'Take a look.'

Jamie aimed them at the trees.
'Wow!' He focused on a flat,
wide dinosaur head with a beak-
shaped snout and let out a low
whistle. 'It's an edmontosaurus—
a real live one!'

CHAPTER 5

Jamie scrambled out of the crater and swept the binoculars along the line of pine trees. 'There's a whole herd of edmontosaurs!' he exclaimed. 'They're massive!'

'Cool,' Tom said, hurrying to join him.

The great lumbering dinosaurs were huddled together at the edge of the forest. They took nervous steps on their hind legs towards the smouldering trees and then skittered back in alarm.

'But they don't belong in the open.'
Tom looked worried. 'That forest must be their home.'

'Looks like they're too scared to go back in,' said Jamie. 'Some of those branches are still on fire.'

He trained the binoculars on an edmontosaurus at the edge of the group and chuckled. 'I think that one's posing for us!'

The eddie lifted its head up and sniffed the air. It opened its mouth, showing rows and rows of flat teeth.

'Those gnashers would make short work
of a tree branch,' Jamie murmured. 'Dad told
me they could have up to a thousand teeth!'

'I wouldn't like to be a dino dentist.' Tom
laughed. 'You'd need a drill the size of a
cricket bat.'

'And buckets of mouthwash.'

'And half your patients would want to eat you!'

'I wish we could get a bit closer,' said Jamie. 'Have we got time?'

Tom looked at his watch. 'Not really. We'd better go. We'll be in big trouble if we're late back for the Grand Opening. Come on, Wanna.'

They began the long walk back towards the geyser crater and the jungle beyond.

'I wish we could tell Dad that we've

seen some real edmontosaurs,' sighed Jamie.
He turned to get one last look at the eddies
and stopped dead.

'Oh no!' he said. 'Look at the flames!
The whole forest is alight now!'

Fierce flickers of fire were shooting up into
the sky from the treetops.

'The eddies don't like it,' said Tom, 'and I
don't blame them. Their home's burning.'

The dinosaurs were backing off from the
trees, buffeting each other in their fear.
The boys could hear their deep anxious calls.

Suddenly a flaming tree
trunk crashed down, hitting the ground in a
shower of sparks.

With a terrified bellow, the herd reared
away and began to run from the burning trees.
Soon the run became a charge. The ground
churned under their pounding feet and dust
flew up round them.

'They're stampeding,' yelled Tom. 'And
they're heading right for us.'

'We better get out of the way, and fast,'
Jamie said. 'Come on, Wanna!'

The boys and their dinosaur friend
sprinted at full speed back the way they had
come, trying to put some distance between
them and the frightened dinosaurs. Soon they

had to dodge the small
fires that still burned here and there
in the blast area from the first meteorite.

Jamie turned to see that the eddies were
still stampeding towards them. 'Wait a minute!'
he shouted. 'If the eddies keep running this
way, they'll fall into the geyser pit.'

Tom slowed down, panting. 'We can't let
that happen!'

'We've got to stop them or turn them away
somehow,' said Jamie.

'We could wave our T-shirts at them,' Tom
suggested.

'Too small,' answered Jamie.

'But we haven't got anything else,' Tom
said, worried.

'Yes, we have,' said Jamie, running over to
a burning bush. 'We'll use fire. That's what
scared them into stampeding in the first
place. We'll stand in front of the pit and wave
burning branches.'

'Brilliant!' said Tom. 'Let's do it.'

Wanna butted their legs as if to keep them
away from the danger.

'No, Wanna,' said Jamie. 'We've got to do
this.' He broke off two crackling branches and
held them high. Wanna backed away,
grunking in alarm. 'Sorry, little friend,'

he said soothingly, 'but it's up to us to save the eddies.'

The boys rushed over to the pit, then turned and faced the oncoming charge.

Jamie could feel sparks from the burning branches stinging his arms but he wasn't going to give up. The terrified edmontosaurs were thundering towards them, churning up the dust.

The drumming of giant hooves was making the ground shudder. Jamie looked over his shoulder to see a large crack appear near his feet.

CRASH!

A great chunk of earth disappeared into the darkness. Now the edge of the pit was right behind them. If the crack got any wider, the boys would fall into the pit themselves.

'The eddies have to stop!' shouted Jamie desperately. 'It's their only chance—and ours!'

Jamie and Tom waved the burning branches as hard as they could.

But the edmontosaurs were surging on, pounding away on all fours. They were so close the boys could see their eyes, wide with fear, and their nostrils flaring in panic.

'It's not working,' cried Tom.

'We can't give up!' Jamie shouted.

The stampeding herd was only metres away now. Was it too late? Were they all going to plunge into the crater?

'STOP!' Jamie and Tom bellowed desperately.

At the last minute, the eddies seemed to notice the fire. The leading dinosaurs reared up in terror and swerved away from the geyser pit. The rest of the herd followed, thundering past, throwing dust into the boys' faces.

'We saved them!' yelled Tom.

Grunk, grunk! Wanna appeared and scampered over.

'I agree, Wanna,' Jamie said. 'That was a close shave.'

'Those eddies used all four legs to gallop,' said Tom. 'No wonder they got up such a speed.'

'That's what we'd better do,' said Jamie, looking at his watch, 'if we're going to be in time for the Grand Opening.'

They hurried back towards the jungle. Wanna was his old self, scurrying between

them, running ahead and grunking happily
all the time.

'At least we got to see a real meteorite,'
said Jamie. 'And you got your wish, Tom.'

'What was that?' Tom was puzzled.

'You wanted to see an edmontosaurus close
up, remember?'

'I didn't mean that close!' Tom grinned.

They climbed back up Gingko Hill.
Wanna waggled his tail in delight as
they went.

'He knows there'll be a nice treat
waiting for him,' Tom added.

When they reached the cave, they took one more look out over Dino World. A herd of triceratops was grazing by the lagoon and hadrosaurs were plodding down to the river by Fang Rock. Pterosaurs lazily circled in the air. They all seemed to know that the danger was over.

'We mustn't forget to change our map when we get back,' said Tom. 'The geysers have gone and there's that new crater. And the eddies' trees, of course.'

Jamie took the binoculars and focused on the eddies' trees which were still burning. 'I hope the fire doesn't spread or we'll be making even more changes.'

'I don't think it will,' said Tom. 'Look.' Away in the distance storm clouds were gathering over the mountains. 'The rain will soon put the fire out.'

The boys hurried into the cave and Wanna followed.

Grunk, grunk! Wanna stared at them sadly for a moment as if he didn't want them to go.

'Don't worry, Wanna,' Tom said, patting him on his hard head. 'We'll be back soon.'

Jamie gave him the last of the gingkoes and Wanna cheered up, gobbling up the treats. Jamie and Tom waved goodbye and stepped backwards into the dinosaur footprints and found themselves back in Dinosaur Cove. They scrambled down to the beach.

Then Tom stopped. 'We can't go to the Grand Opening like this. We're filthy.'

'You're right. Grandad will have a fit,' said Jamie, 'and I don't know what Dad will do—explode probably.'

'Quick,' said Tom. 'We'll have a wash in the sea.'

They hurriedly scrubbed the grime off their arms, legs, and faces and made a dash for the lighthouse. The distant church clock was striking one.

It looked as if the whole village had come to the Grand Opening, and crowds of tourists too. A queue stretched away down the path.

'Our clothes will have to do,' muttered Jamie as they made their way past the line of people. 'We've got no more time. Hopefully everyone will be too busy looking at the museum to notice.'

Then they heard a loud voice. 'That edmontosaurus would be an easy target!' A boy of about fifteen was looking at a poster for the museum, showing the eddie model. He seemed to be telling his friend all about dinosaurs. 'They were slow plodders, believe me. Anything could eat them if they wanted. Bet they couldn't run.'

'Are you sure?' his friend asked.

'Of course I'm sure,' said the boy. 'I know everything there is to know about dinosaurs.'

Tom looked at Jamie. 'You tell him,' he whispered.

'Excuse me,' said Jamie politely. 'But the edmontosaurus could get up quite a speed by running on all four legs. It wasn't always an easy target.'

'How do you know?' demanded the boy.

'I've seen—' Jamie stopped himself and quickly recovered. 'I've seen the edmontosaurus skeleton inside. Have a look when you go in. Its front limbs were definitely long enough to run on.'

The boy stared at him open-mouthed.

Tom and Jamie saw Grandad waving them over. They marched up to the front of the queue and up onto the little stage to stand with Jamie's dad.

'Welcome to the Dinosaur Cove Museum,' Mr Morgan began. 'The most magical dinosaur place in the whole world . . .'

Jamie smiled a huge smile. He was proud of his dad's new museum but nothing compared to Dino World.

'The second most magical place,' Jamie whispered to Tom.

DINOSAUR WORLD

BOYS' ROUTE

Jungle

Misty Lagoon

White Ocean

76

Far Away Mountains

Crashing
Rock
Falls

Great Plains

Fang
Rock

Gingko
Hill

GLOSSARY

Ammonite (am-on-ite) – an extinct animal with octopus-like legs and often a spiral-shaped shell that lived in the ocean.

Edmontosaurus (ed-mon-tow-sor-us) – a plant-eating, usually slow-moving dinosaur that walked on its back two legs. Named after the place it was discovered in southern Alberta, Canada, once called 'Lower Edmonton'.

Geyser (gee-ser) – a hot spring, heated by volcanic activity below the earth's surface, that erupts in a tall stream of hot water and steam, sometimes on a regular schedule.

Gingko (gink-oh) – a tree native to China called a 'living fossil' because fossils of it have been found dating back millions of years, yet they are still around today. Also known as the stink bomb tree because of its smelly apricot-like fruit.

Hadrosaur (had-ro-sor) – a duck-billed dinosaur. This plant eater had a toothless beak but hundreds of teeth in their cheeks.

Meteor (meet-e-or) – matter from outer space that glows when falling through the earth's atmosphere.

Meteorite (meet-e-or-ite) – a meteor that lands on the earth's surface.

Pterosaur (ter-oh-sor) – a prehistoric flying reptile. Its wings were leathery and light and some of these 'winged lizards' had fur on their bodies and bony crests on their heads.

Triceratops (T-tops) (try-serra-tops) – a three-horned, plant-eating dinosaur which looks like a rhinoceros.

Wannanosaurus (wah-nan-oh-sor-us) – a dinosaur that only ate plants and used its hard, flat skull to defend itself. Named after the place it was discovered: Wannano in China.

Come and meet me...
in a Jurassic adventure